W9-CEJ-917

Brad the Wonder Baby

DI BATES

Illustrated by Luke Jurevicius

The Story Characters

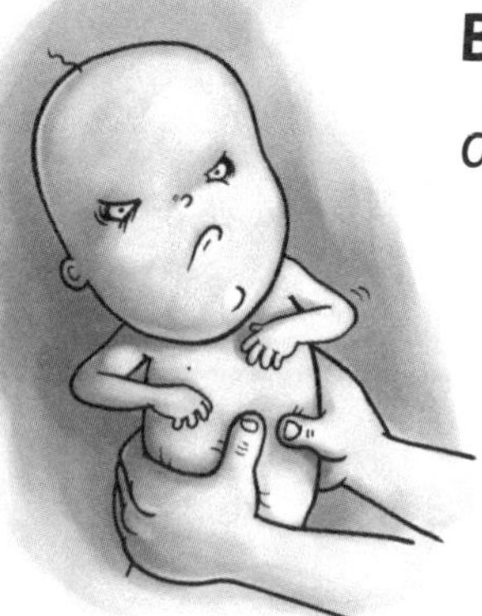

Brad Crumble

did not like being born.

Sophie Crumble

had a big secret.

Mom and Dad Crumble

are Brad and Sophie's parents.

The Story Setting

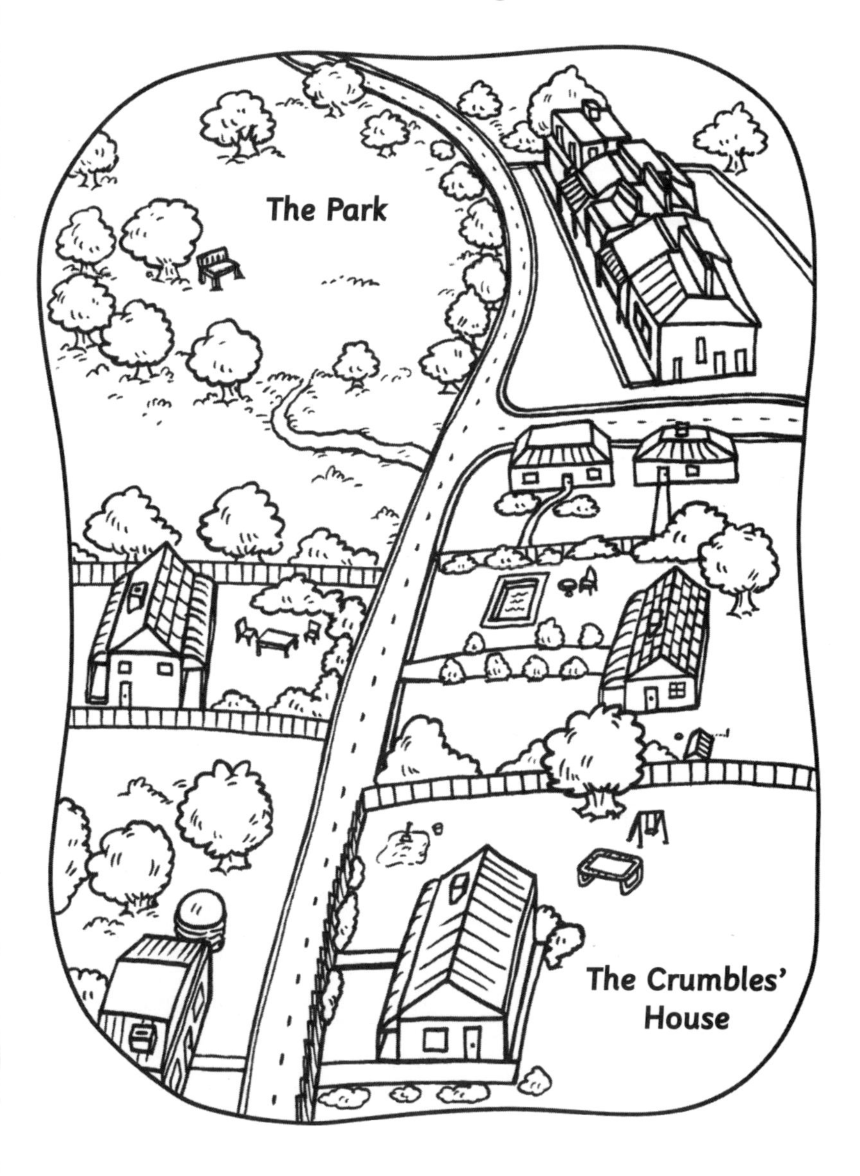

Brad Meets His Family

Brad Crumble did not like being born. A doctor slapped his bottom. Someone fiddled with his belly button. Bright lights hurt his eyes.

Brad did not like the hospital. The other babies slept or cried. No one wanted to talk or play. He was bored.

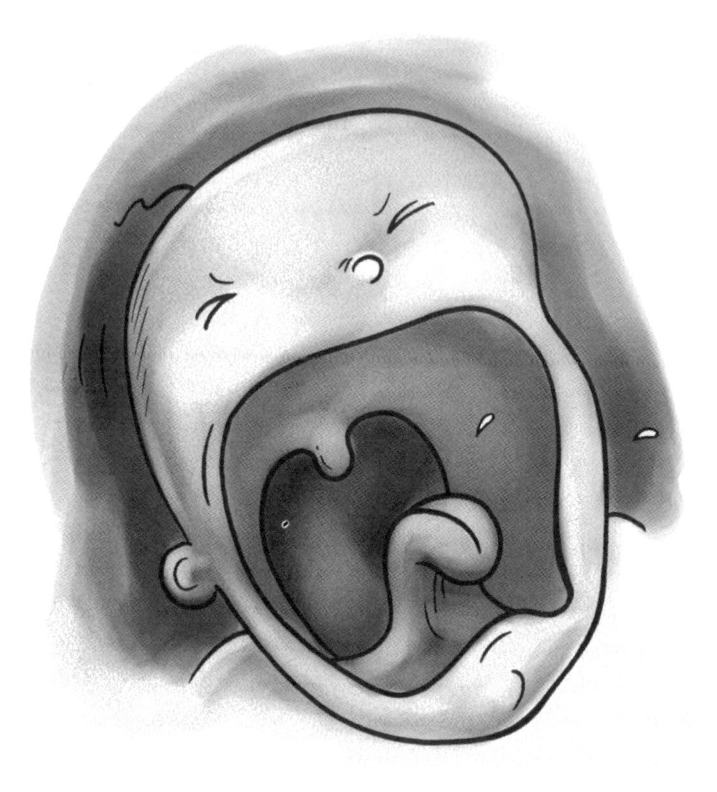

Mom and Dad were no fun.
"Goo," said Dad.

"Gah," said Mom.
"Kitchy, kitchy, koo."

Brad yelled at them to speak English.
His parents only heard "Waaaaaah!"

"He's got a good set of lungs," said his dad.

"He's hungry," said his mom.

"He's cute," said his sister Sophie.

Brad Can Fly

On Brad's first night at home, he threw off his blanket. "OK!" he said, flapping his arms. "Now for some real fun."

He flew up to the ceiling. Zap! Just like that.

"Wow," he said. "This is great!" He looked down at his room.

Brad flapped his arms again. Down he zoomed. Zoom! Just like that.

“What fun,” Brad said.

He flapped again, and up he flew.

He flipped

and dipped.

He whizzed

and whirled.

He twisted

and curled.

Up to the ceiling, down to the floor, across to the wall he flew. “Yippee!” he cried.

Oh no! Footsteps! Someone was walking down the hall. Brad flew back into his crib. He dived under his blanket and closed his eyes.

The door opened. The baby's asleep, Dad thought. He yawned and went back down the hall to bed.

Brad waited. After a while he heard
ZZZZZZZZZZZZZZZ.
Dad was snoring.

ZZZZZZZZZZZZZZZZZZ.
So was Mom.

ZZZZZZZZZZ.

So was his sister Sophie.

“They’re all asleep. Now I can explore,” said Brad.

Brad Flies Outside

Brad flew around and around in his room. He flew in circles until he got so dizzy that he started to cry.

Then Brad flew out of his room. He was off to explore the house.

It was dark. Brad couldn't see much. And he didn't know how to turn on the lights.

Brad could see light coming in through the window. He could see houses, trees, and cars outside the window.

Brad wanted to go outside. The living room window was open. Swish went the curtains as Brad flew past them.

Above the roof he zoomed. He was so high! By the light of the moon, he could see the backyard. It had a swing and a trampoline.

Brad flew down to find out what each thing did. He tried to land on the trampoline. He bounced into the air. "Wheeee!" squealed Brad.

He bounced again.
He flipped
and dipped.
He twisted
and curled.
Brad giggled and squealed.

Brad Almost Gets Caught

When the person next door opened the back door, Brad whizzed up into a tall tree. He didn't want anyone to know that he could fly.

He sat on a branch and watched. The man stood at his back door. He looked into the darkness. He shined a flashlight into his backyard.

The flashlight shined in Brad's eyes. Oh no! The man would see him! The man walked into the backyard. He came closer and closer.

"Is there anyone out there, Bill?" a woman's voice called from inside the house.

"There's no one out here, dear," the man said. He went back inside.

Then Brad saw the scariest thing. Two eyes were floating in the air above him. Brad's heart beat hard in his chest.

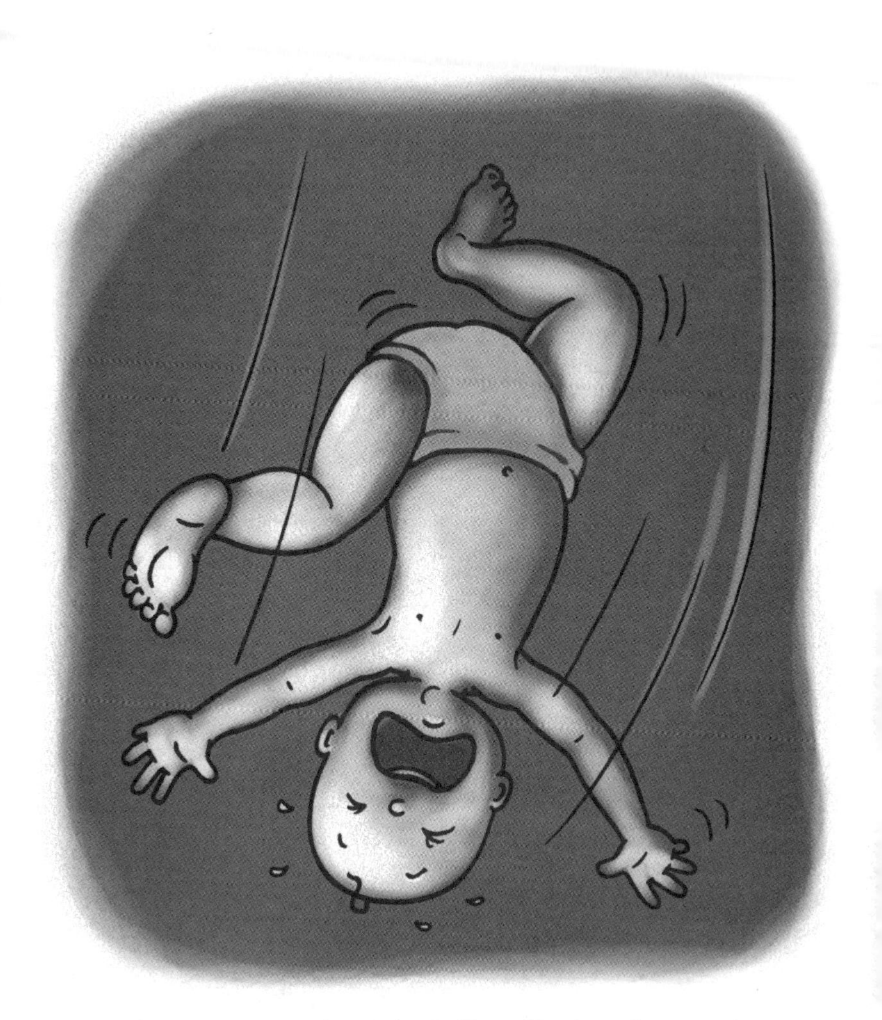

Brad screamed. He fell off the branch.
Down he fell,
down,
down,
down.

Brad was just about to hit the ground.
Then he remembered that he could fly.
He flapped his arms and flew up.

He flew up to another tree. He had to zoom away from the scary eyes that said, "Hoot! Hoot!"

Chapter 5

Brad Meets a Monster

Brad should have gone home, but he was having fun. He flew onto a nearby roof. He looked down the chimney. He slid down the roof tiles.

Brad looked down into this new backyard. Near the back fence was a little house. Brad flew down to take a closer look.

The house was dark and shadowy. Something was asleep inside. Brad reached out and touched its nose. The thing with a cold, wet nose woke up. "Grrr . . . "

Brad flew away as fast as he could.

"Woof! Woof! Woof!"

The sounds of the loud barks cut through the night.

A light went on in Brad's house.
"Uh-oh!" said Brad. "I'd better get back before Mom and Dad get up."

Brad flew back to his room. When his mom looked in on him, Brad was fast asleep.

Chapter 6

Brad and Sophie

Brad loved his sister Sophie. She spent lots of time with him. She talked to him. She didn't say "goo, goo" or "kitchy, kitchy, koo."

Sophie told him stories and sang songs to him. She patted him on the back when he had a pain in his belly. She stroked Brad's head when he couldn't sleep.

“I have a really big secret,” Sophie whispered in Brad’s ear. “No one in the whole world knows my secret. Maybe one day I will tell you.”

Brad wanted to tell Sophie his secret. Sophie seemed to be just the right person, but Brad wasn't sure, yet.

One day Brad saw a flashlight on top of the fridge. That night Brad flew into the kitchen and picked up the flashlight.

He took the flashlight with him on his trip to the park. He shined the flashlight on everything he saw. He looked inside store windows. He woke up sleeping dogs.

On this trip, some people saw Brad!

Brad's Secret Is Discovered

"I've seen a flying saucer," a man told the police.

“I must be seeing things,” said a lady.
“I’ll have to get my eyes tested.”

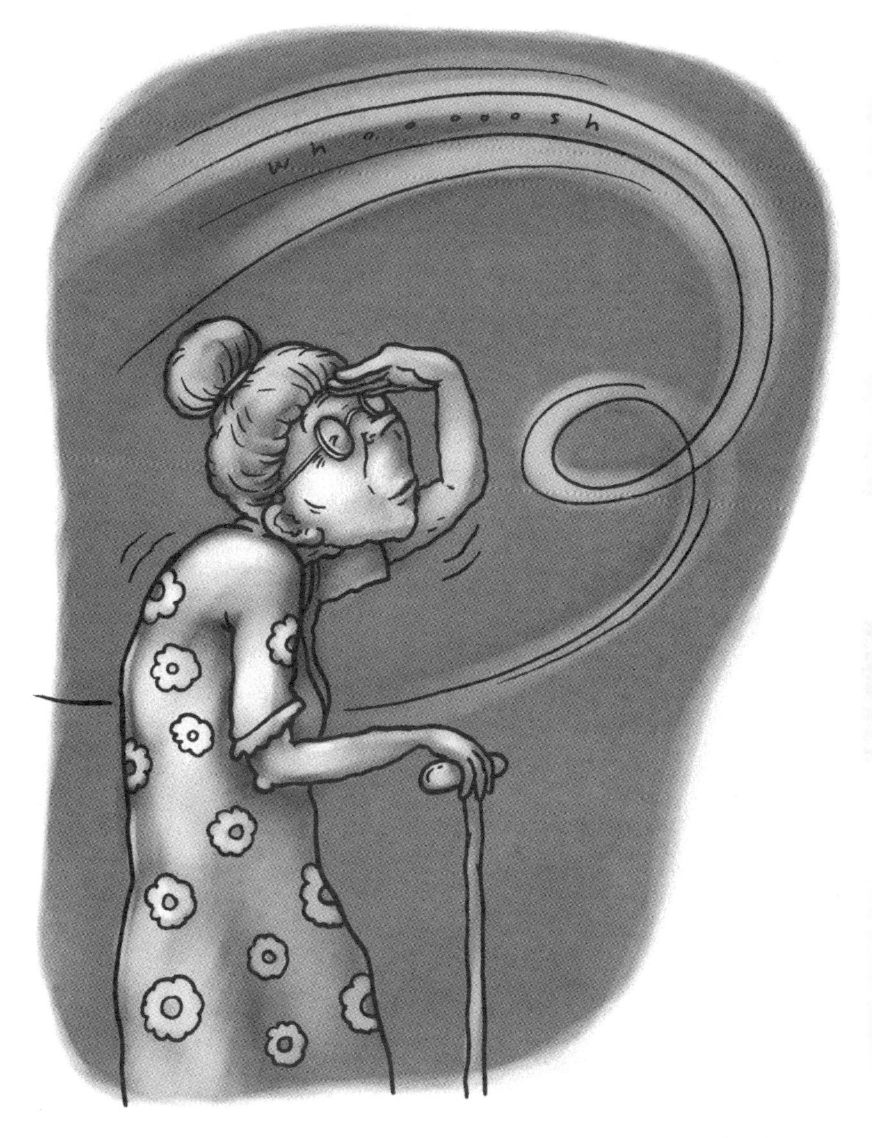

A man gazing at the sky saw Brad. "Was that a flying baby with a flashlight?" he yelled. "I must be dreaming!"

Brad flew home. He was about to go in the window when he saw someone inside. They had a flashlight, too!

"Oh no!" said Brad. "What will I do?"

Brad pressed his face against the window to see who it was. He couldn't see at first. Was it Mom? Was it Dad? Maybe it was a stranger! A burglar? Brad was scared.

The flashlight was moving. It was going up and up. It went higher until it was almost at the ceiling!

Brad was so surprised that he banged his flashlight against the window.

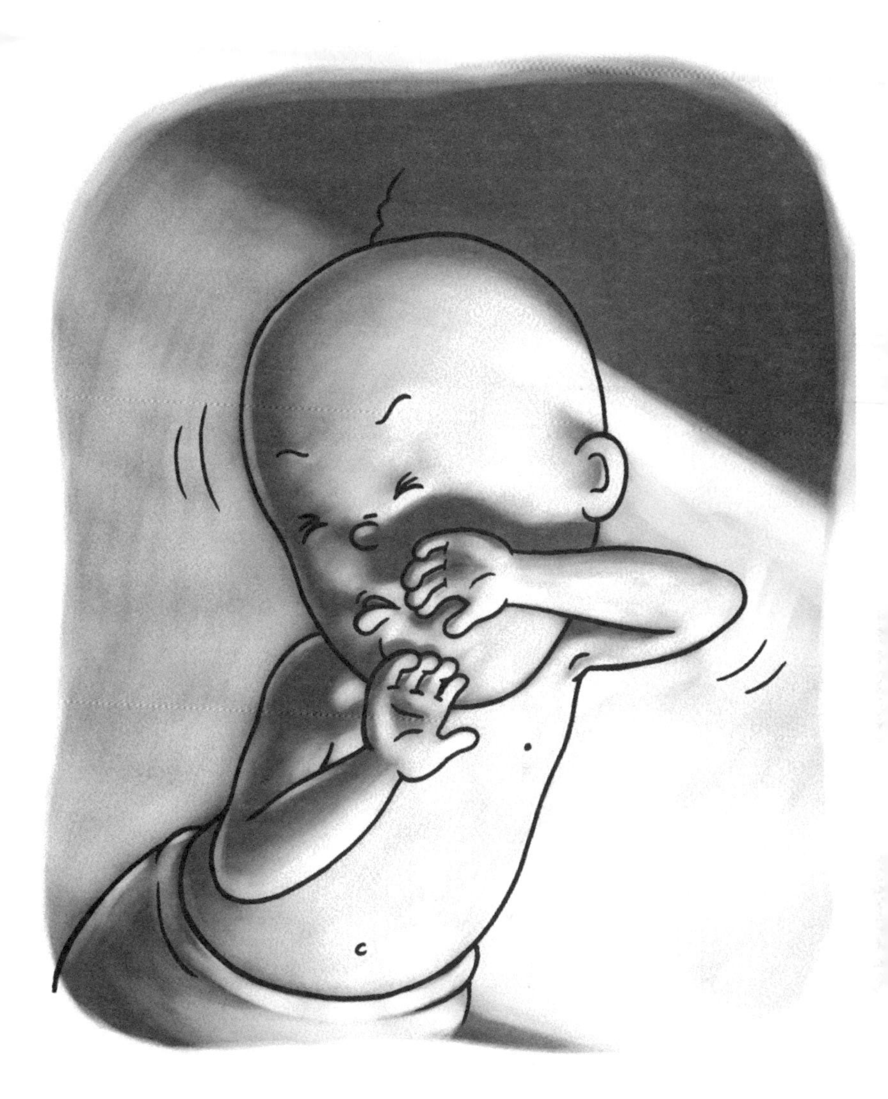

The beam from the other flashlight shined onto Brad. The light blinded him. He had been seen!

“Brad!” It was his sister Sophie. She dropped the flashlight she was holding to the floor.

Brad was so happy to see Sophie that he flew right into her arms.

“You can fly!” Sophie sounded amazed. “This is the most incredible thing in the world!”

Now Brad knew Sophie's big secret.
She could fly, too!

“I thought I was the only person in the world who could fly,” whispered Sophie. “But you can fly, too! Brad, we are going to have such fun!”

From then on, the two of them went flying together. They had great fun, but they never told anyone their secret.

To this day, no one knows Brad and Sophie's secret . . . except you!

Glossary

amazed

very surprised

ceiling

the top part of a room

dizzy

when your head spins

explore

to look around a new place

flying saucer
a spaceship shaped
like a saucer

snoring
making loud noises
while sleeping

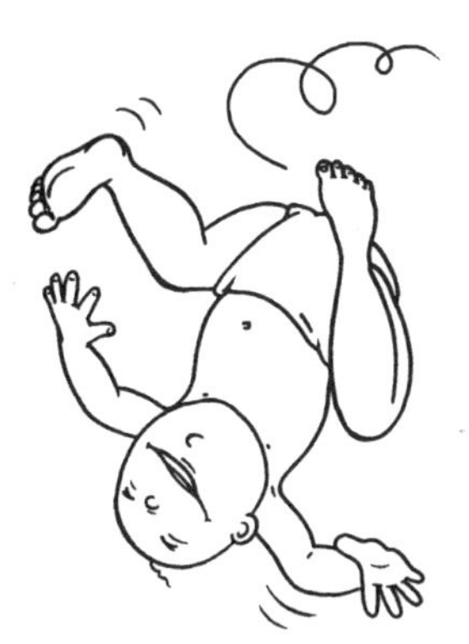

whirled
tumbled around and around

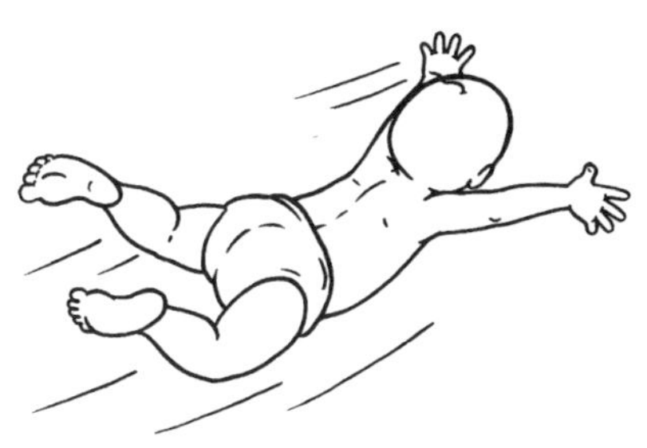

whizzed
moved in a big rush

Talking with the Author and the Illustrator

Di Bates (author)

If you could go anywhere, where would it be?

I would go back in time to my tenth birthday.

Why is the sky blue?

Because that's the best color to form a background for the birds of the world.

What are three things that you can't live without?

My husband Bill Condon, water, and a pen.

Luke Jurevicius (illustrator)

If you could go anywhere, where would it be?

I would go to an island in the tropics.

Why is the sky blue?

Because all the colors had a vote and blue won.

What are three things that you can't live without?

My music, my close friends, and the truth.

sundance™

Copyright © 2002 Sundance/Newbridge, LLC

All rights reserved. No part of this publication may be reproduced, stored in a retrieval system or transmitted in any form or by any means, electronic, mechanical,photocopying, recording, or otherwise, without the prior written permission of the publisher.

Published by Sundance Publishing
33 Boston Post Road West, Suite 440, Marlborough, MA 01752
800-343-8204

Copyright © text Di Bates
Copyright © illustrations Luke Jurevicius

First published 1999 as Sparklers by
Blake Education, Locked Bag 2022, Glebe 2037, Australia
Exclusive United States Distribution: Sundance Publishing

ISBN 978-0-7608-5137-1

Printed by Nordica International Ltd.
Manufactured in Guangzhou, China
May, 2010
Nordica Job#: 05-53-10
Sundance/Newbridge PO#: 225991